Looking at differences between . . .

FAIR GROVE
LIBRARY

$20.00

Using Graphic Organizers to Study the Living Environment™

Looking at Differences Between Living and Nonliving Things with Graphic Organizers

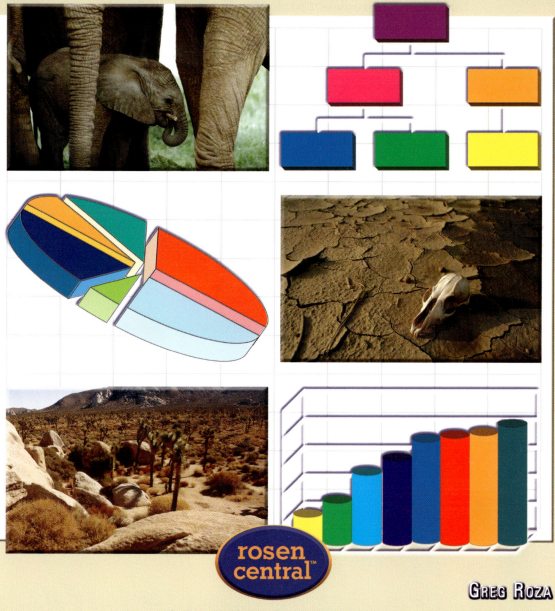

rosen central™

Greg Roza

The Rosen Publishing Group, Inc., New York

For Willie and Laurie

Published in 2006 by The Rosen Publishing Group, Inc.
29 East 21st Street, New York, NY 10010

Copyright © 2006 by The Rosen Publishing Group, Inc.

First Edition

All rights reserved. No part of this book may be reproduced in any form without permission in writing from the publisher, except by a reviewer.

Library of Congress Cataloging-in-Publication Data

Roza, Greg.
Looking at differences between living and nonliving things with graphic organizers/Greg Roza.—1st ed.
  p. cm.—(Using graphic organizers to study the living environment)
Includes bibliographical references.
ISBN 1-4042-0611-6 (library binding)
1. Biology—Study and teaching (Elementary)—Graphic methods—Juvenile literature.
I. Title. II. Series.
QH315.R69 2006
372.35'7—dc22

2005017392

Manufactured in the United States of America

On the cover: A bar chart *(top right)*, a pie chart *(center)*, and a flow chart *(bottom left)*.

Contents

Introduction 4

Chapter One Cells: The Fundamental Units of Life 7

Chapter Two The Processes of Life 14

Chapter Three Plants 22

Chapter Four Animals 28

Chapter Five The Balance of Nature 36

Glossary 42

For More Information 44

For Further Reading 45

Bibliography 46

Index 47

Introduction

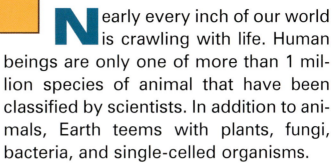

Nearly every inch of our world is crawling with life. Human beings are only one of more than 1 million species of animal that have been classified by scientists. In addition to animals, Earth teems with plants, fungi, bacteria, and single-celled organisms.

What is it that allows us to remain alive? Living things and nonliving things alike are both made of the same atoms. So what sets living things apart from nonliving things? For one, living things are much more complex than nonliving things. However, we've just scratched the surface of biology, or the study of living things, by asking this question. The subject of biology can teach us so much about Earth's abundance of life. The subject can be an interesting and even amazing topic. But like so many other scientific topics, biology can also seem a bit overwhelming at times. Lucky for you, you can use graphic organizers to aid you in gaining a better understanding of the topic of biology and the differences between living and nonliving things.

Earth is a place of great diversity. There are so many different species of living things that we literally are finding new species every day. However, Earth contains an abundance of nonliving things, too, on which life depends. These nonliving things include water, oxygen, and nutrients.

Looking at Differences Between Living and Nonliving Things with Graphic Organizers

Graphic organizers are diagrams that illustrate a concept in visual form. They are helpful in many ways. They guide you as you learn about a topic, using illustrations, graphics, and text to help you remember information. Graphic organizers often simplify information so it is easier to recall. They are also valuable tools in developing test-taking skills because they provide a map of information that can be read, reread, and remembered when it really counts. Perhaps most important, graphic organizers help make a potentially difficult topic easier to understand.

There's no simple answer to the question, "What is life?" However, we can use graphic organizers to better understand what it means to be alive. We can also use them to gain a better understanding of the complex interactions between living things and nonliving things on planet Earth.

Chapter One

Cells: The Fundamental Units of Life

All living things have cells. These tiny units of life set living things apart from nonliving things. Cells carry out the life processes necessary to keep an organism alive. To truly understand those processes, it is important to have a basic understanding of what cells are and how they function.

Cell Theory

In 1665, an English physicist named Robert Hooke made one of the first compound microscopes, which are microscopes with two or more lenses. While looking at a thin slice of cork through his microscope, he realized that it was not solid. It was made of many tiny compartments that he called cells. The word "cell" comes

Cell Diagram

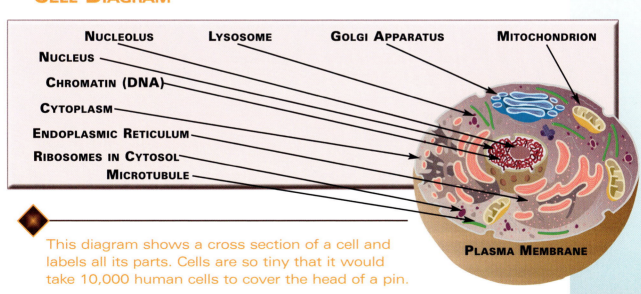

This diagram shows a cross section of a cell and labels all its parts. Cells are so tiny that it would take 10,000 human cells to cover the head of a pin.

from the Latin word *cella*, which means "storeroom" or "small container." These compartments were the empty remains of plant cells. A human being had never seen something so small before.

In 1674, a Dutch man named Antonie van Leeuwenhoek used a microscope that he had made to discover that there is a miniature world teeming with life all around (and on) us.

Timeline Chart: Cell Theory

1665	English physicist Robert Hooke creates the first compound microscope. Using this microscope, Hooke is the first person to see the cellular structure of plant tissue. Hooke coins the name "cell" to describe the tiny compartments he sees in a thin slice of cork.
1674	Dutch scientist Antonie van Leeuwenhoek, using a microscope that he made, is the first person to see bacteria, red blood cells, protozoa, and numerous other single-celled organisms.
1838	German botanist Matthias Schleiden observes that all plants are made of cells. German physiologist Theodor Schwann observes that all animals are made of cells.
1839	German physiologist Theodor Schwann publishes his theory that all living things are made of cells.
1858	German psychologist Rudolf Virchow reveals that we get sick because our cells get sick.

This is a timeline chart. A timeline chart illustrates a series of events in the order in which they occurred. Here specifically, we have a timeline of the groundbreaking events in cell theory.

CELLS: THE FUNDAMENTAL UNITS OF LIFE

In 1838, German botanist Matthias Schleiden observed that all plants are made of cells. That same year, German physiologist Theodor Schwann made the same assertion regarding animals. Schwann published his ideas about cells in 1839 and was the first to state that all living creatures, plants and animals, are made of a cell or cells and that cells are tiny units of life.

Today, Schleiden and Schwann are both credited with founding cell theory. Yet each of these science pioneers aided in establishing modern cell theory. Since their time, there have been many significant discoveries regarding cells. Today, the cell theory has six main principles, as seen in this graphic organizer.

RANKING CHART: CELL THEORY RANKING

THE SIX MAIN PRINCIPLES OF CELL THEORY

1. ALL LIVING THINGS ARE MADE OF CELLS.
2. THE CELL IS THE BASIC UNIT OF LIFE.
3. CELLS ONLY ARISE FROM PREEXISTING CELLS.
4. CELLS CONTAIN HEREDITARY INFORMATION THAT IS PASSED ON TO NEW CELLS.
5. ALL CELLS ARE MADE UP OF THE SAME CHEMICALS.
6. MANY LIFE-SUSTAINING CHEMICAL REACTIONS TAKE PLACE IN CELLS.

A ranking chart places events in order of rank. Rank, however, can be defined in a number of ways. You might rank a series of events from first occurrence to last occurrence or from most important to least important, the way this cell theory–ranking chart is organized.

What Do Cells Do?

Once scientists knew that the cell was the basic unit of life, they wanted to know how cells worked. They aimed their microscopes ever deeper, prying into the inner world of the cell itself. Scientists once thought that cells were filled with a single, basic fluid they called protoplasm. It wasn't until the electron microscope was invented that scientists discovered that cells are filled with complex organelles floating in a fluid called cytoplasm. Organelles are similar to the organs of the body in that each one fulfills specific life processes. Organelles often work together to carry out these processes. The cell is enclosed in a membrane that forms a barrier between it and its surroundings. The membrane allows beneficial materials—such as protein and oxygen—to pass into the cell while keeping out harmful substances. The membrane also allows waste to leave the cell.

Cells are like little factories that churn away all the time, processing materials and creating energy. Cell activity is governed by chemical reactions. The activities that take place within cells are the reason that life exists. Nearly all animal cells have the same basic design. Likewise, all plant cells are similar in structure and function. However, there are several key differences between plant cells and animal cells.

Animal Cells

Nearly every animal cell type has a control center called a nucleus. Chromosomes within the nucleus are tiny structures that contain genes, which is the biological blueprint that is inherited by offspring. The nucleus also controls the growth and development of the cell. Outside of the nucleus float numerous organelles, each with its own specific job.

The endoplasmic reticulum is a tube-shaped organelle that is attached to the nucleus. Its main job is to transport nutrients throughout the cell and between cells, but the production of protein also occurs on its surface. The Golgi bodies (or Golgi apparatus) process proteins made by the endoplasmic reticulum, wrapping it up in packages called vesicles. These vesicles move to the cell membrane and release their contents outside of the cell. Mitochondria release the energy from food during the process of cellular respiration. Lysosomes use enzymes to break large molecules into smaller ones. Tiny vacuoles provide storage for materials and support for the cell. These and other organelles use chemical reactions to work together in a similar way to how our organs work together.

Plant Cells

Plant cells are similar to animal cells in many ways. Most of the organelles are the same or very similar to those in animal cells. There are, however, several key differences that biologists look at

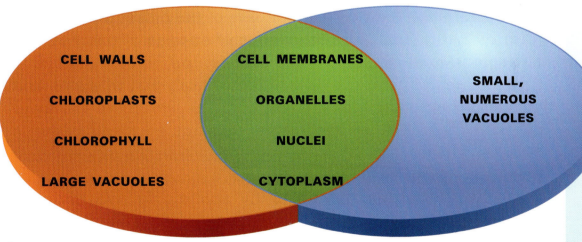

Venn Diagram: Plant Cells and Animal Cells

A Venn diagram illustrates what one set of properties has in common with another set of properties. In this Venn diagram, we see the unique properties of plant and animal cells in separate circles. The area of overlap shows what properties plants and animals have in common.

when determining how to classify new species. Plant cells have organelles called chloroplasts. Chloroplasts contain a green pigment called chlorophyll, which gives plants their green appearance. This pigment allows plants to use sunlight to change water and carbon dioxide into food. This process, called photosynthesis, is vital to life on Earth. Oxygen is a waste product of photosynthesis. Animal cells combine oxygen and food to create energy, with carbon dioxide being the waste product.

In addition to a cell membrane, plant cells have the more rigid cell wall, which is made primarily of a nonliving substance called cellulose. The cell wall provides protection for the cell and helps support the plant as a whole. Plants also have very large vacuoles, whereas animal cells generally have small vacuoles.

Single-Celled Organisms

Plants and animals were once thought to be the only two forms of life. The advent of the microscope allowed scientists to see what makes them different at the most basic level. It also revealed an invisible world teeming with single-celled life.

Bacteria are the simplest and one of the oldest types of lifeform on Earth. There are thousands of species of bacteria, but all bacteria exist as one of three shapes: rod, round, and spiral. Bacterial cell structure is very different from that of plants and animals. Their organelles are less complex, and there are fewer of them. The DNA of bacteria is also not enclosed within a nucleus. Instead, the DNA floats freely within the single-celled creature—creatures whose cells lack a nucleus are known as prokaryotic. Bacteria reproduce by splitting in two during a process called cell division. Some bacteria use a simple means of locomotion, usually minute hairs called flagella that function somewhat like oars.

Until the 1970s, scientists thought single-celled archaea were bacteria. Now they are understood to be very different creatures. Many scientists believe that bacteria and archaea evolved from a

CELLS: THE FUNDAMENTAL UNITS OF LIFE

BACTERIUM DIAGRAM

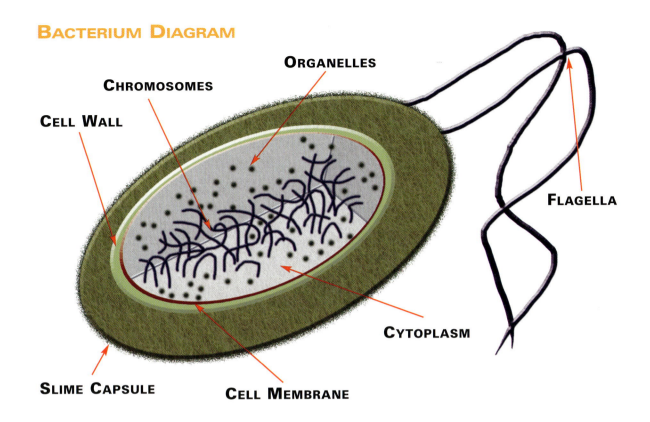

One type of graphic organizer is a simple diagram. A diagram, such as the one here, illustrates and labels each part of an object. This is a diagram of a bacterium.

similar ancestor more than 3.5 billion years ago. Archaea are generally found in extreme conditions, such as in the boiling water of geysers and the waters of Earth's saltiest seas.

The term "protist" refers to a wide variety of interesting creatures that can be both single-celled and multicelled. All protists are eukaryotic, which means that their cells contain a nucleus. Protists fall into one of two categories: algae and protozoa. Protozoa feed on bacteria, other protozoa, and tiny bits of organic material. The amoeba is one of the most interesting of all the single-celled creatures. The cell wall around an amoeba is very flexible. Amoebas move by oozing forward. They attack their prey by engulfing and digesting it.

Chapter Two

The Processes of Life

Our world is filled with a breathtaking array of living things. Because of such a variety, scientists have developed a system of scientific classification, called the taxonomy table, which names each and every type of living creature.

The largest of the groups in the taxonomy table is the kingdom. Though the table originally had only two kingdoms, most scientists today agree that there are five kingdoms: Animalia, Plantae, Fungi, Protista (protozoa and algae), and

Inverted Triangle: Scientific Classification

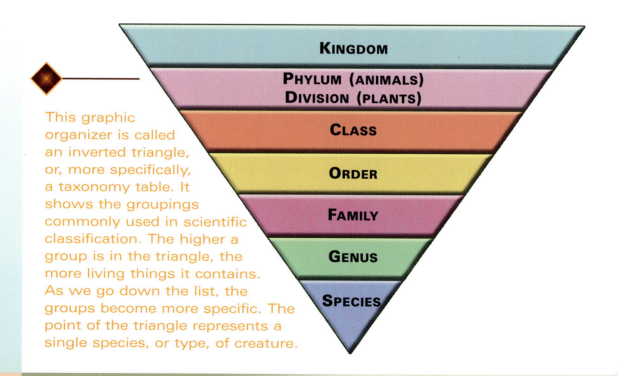

This graphic organizer is called an inverted triangle, or, more specifically, a taxonomy table. It shows the groupings commonly used in scientific classification. The higher a group is in the triangle, the more living things it contains. As we go down the list, the groups become more specific. The point of the triangle represents a single species, or type, of creature.

Monera (bacteria). All living things belong to one of these five kingdoms. The farther a category gets from its kingdom in the scientific classification, the more specific its description.

The taxonomy table is a valuable tool in biology. It helps to reduce confusion when discussing living things. It also makes it easier for scientists to see the evolutionary connections between different organisms. With many millions of organisms in the world, scientists need all the help they can get!

There are so many different species of living things in this world, as illustrated above, that it would be impossible to study all of them without a classification system. Taxonomy organizes each category of organism into one of five kingdoms. From there, each species is classified into various subcategories.

What Is Life?

No matter how different all of the living things in our world seem, they all share eight basic traits, seven of which are called life processes. These basic traits include nutrition, transport, respiration, synthesis and growth, excretion, regulation, reproduction, and movement. These eight traits are common to all living things, no matter how different they may appear.

Many nonliving things may exhibit one or more of these characteristics, but in order to be classified as living, they would have to exhibit all eight. Crystals are minerals that are capable of growth. Viruses, once inside an organism, carry out metabolic processes with the aid of living cells. Once a virus is removed from a cell, it dies. For this reason, scientists don't consider viruses living things. A gas heater has a thermostat that allows the man-made machine to regulate its functions, turning on when it is cold and shutting off

Concept Web: Eight Traits of Living Things

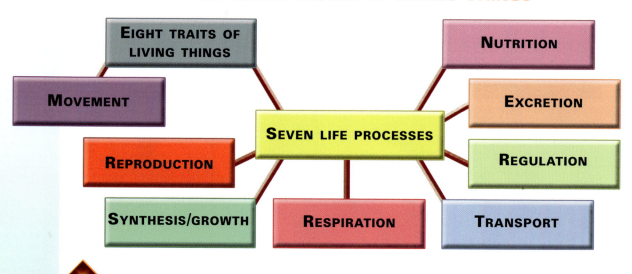

This word web shows the eight traits of living things. Notice that seven of these traits are called life processes, and they make up a different part of the web than movement. This shows that movement is not necessary for life to exist.

when it is hot. However, one life process does not make something alive. Let's take a closer look at each of these characteristics of life.

NUTRITION

Nutrition is the life process by which living things obtain energy. As the term suggests, this usually involves taking in nutrients from the environment. Without energy, living things would not be able to carry out the other life processes. They also wouldn't be able to move around, communicate, or simply remain alive.

TRANSPORT

Transport is the process by which materials are distributed to organs within the living thing. This life process can occur across cell membranes, within cells, and between the different parts of an organism. Transport is essential to achieving a balance of chemicals within an organism.

RESPIRATION

Respiration is the life process of releasing the energy stored in food. This is accomplished by combining oxygen with the food. Organisms need energy in order to grow, reproduce, move, and stay alive.

SYNTHESIS AND GROWTH

Many people consider these as two different life processes, but they both deal with the increase in size of a living thing. Synthesis is the life process by which the cells in a living thing use chemical reactions to combine small molecules obtained from nutrition into larger molecules. These larger molecules are often used to form the parts of cells. This helps to rebuild worn or damaged cells, or to create completely new cells.

Growth is the life process by which living things increase in size. Growth is a direct result of synthesis. Single-celled organisms grow because synthesis makes the cell larger. Multicelled organisms grow due to the increase in the number of cells created during synthesis.

EXCRETION

The chemical reactions that take place within cells produce a variety of waste materials. These materials could be harmful to a living thing if they are allowed to build up within the cells. Excretion is the life process by which cellular waste products are removed from the organism. This life process should not be confused with the elimination of solid wastes from the body, which is a function of nutrition.

REGULATION

Regulation is the life process that a living thing uses to control and coordinate its life processes. Regulation is an organism's way of responding to environmental changes, called stimuli, that could otherwise be life-threatening. Without regulation, an organism would be incapable of maintaining a stable internal environment. This would ultimately lead to illness and death. For example, regulation allows mammals to maintain a constant body temperature. Human beings get a fever—or a rise in body temperature—when they are ill. A fever is the result of a body defending itself against infection.

REPRODUCTION

Reproduction is the life process by which living things create new individuals. It is the only life process that is not necessary for the survival of the organism, but it is necessary for the survival of the species. Sexual reproduction involves the joining of two cells from two different parents. This results in wide varieties of living creatures because of the combination of two sets of chromosomes. Many creatures reproduce via asexual reproduction, which only requires one parent. Single-celled creatures often reproduce by cell division, which creates two identical organisms. Other creatures, like the hydra (a simple animal), reproduce asexually through budding. This means that an offspring develops right on the parent's body and breaks away after it has matured.

The Processes of Life

Reproduction is vital to life. During reproduction, the parent organisms pass on their genetic material in the form of chromosomes to the new organism. Nearly every type of cell carries

Comparison Matrix: Reproduction

	\\ CHARACTERISTICS						
	Plants and Animals	Human Beings	Single-Celled Organisms	2 Parents	1 Parent	Exchange of Genetic Material	Asexual Reproduction
Sexual Reproduction	X	X		X		X	
Budding	X				X	X	X
Cell Division			X		X	X	X

This graphic organizer is called a comparison matrix. A comparison matrix forms a grid, from which you can compare and analyze traits of the groups specified in a clear and concise way. Here, we can see what characteristics the different types of reproduction have.

chromosomes, which contain the information that makes each creature a unique individual.

Movement

Although it cannot be considered a life process, most scientists agree that all living things exhibit some form of movement. Most animals have developed a system of locomotion that enables

Looking at Differences Between Living and Nonliving Things with Graphic Organizers

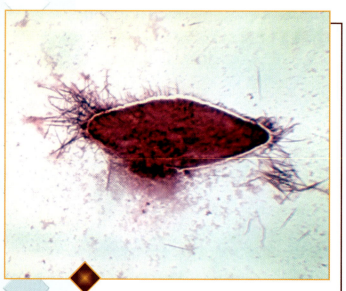

Paramecia, like the one shown here, are about the size of the period at the end of this sentence. The nail-shaped protrusions on the surface of this paramecium are called trichocysts, which are believed to be anchoring devices.

them to move from one place to another. Complex animals have muscles, bones, and brains that allow them to move legs, arms, wings, and tails.

We may think of plants as immobile beings, but all plants are able to move, and some in very unusual ways. Growth is one form of movement. Green, leafy plants use a unique system to turn their leaves and flowers to face the sun. As the prairie tumbleweed dies, it dries up and breaks away from its root, allowing it to spread its seeds as it tumbles away with the wind.

Even single-celled creatures are capable of moving. Paramecia have tiny "hairs" called cilia that they wave about, allowing them to move. Amoeba ooze parts of their unicellular bodies forward, and the rest follows soon after.

METABOLISM

As we've seen, the cells and organs of an organism have a lot of work to do to remain alive. An organism depends on a wide range of chemicals and chemical reactions in order to stay healthy. These chemical reactions make the life processes possible. The sum total of an organism's chemical reactions is known as its metabolism. There are two types of metabolism: anabolism and catabolism. During anabolism, cells build new organic materials from smaller molecules. During catabolism, cells tear down organic materials, releasing energy in the process.

Homeostasis

In order for a living thing to function properly, it must keep its inner environment as stable as possible. This is sometimes difficult due to effects the external environment imposes on the organism. All living things must keep their internal systems stable, regardless of changes to the external environment. This stability is known as homeostasis, which literally means "same condition." Although it is the life process of regulation that allows an organism to achieve homeostasis, homeostasis is a result of all of the life processes working together. A lack of homeostasis can endanger the life of the organism. For example, humans can get sick or die if our bodies get too hot or too cold. Such would be the lack of homeostasis.

Sandwich Chart

Metabolism is the sum total of an organism's reactions.

An organism depends on a wide range of chemicals and chemical reactions to remain healthy.

Chemical reactions take place within cells.

During anabolism, cells build new organic materials from smaller molecules.

During catabolism, cells tear down organic materials, releasing energy in the process.

Chemical reactions make the life processes possible.

A sandwich chart, such as the one above, breaks down a concept into its component parts. The top and bottom pieces of bread in the sandwich are the grand themes of the concept.

Chapter Three

Plants

hile all organisms sustain life with the same life processes, these processes often appear very different from one type of organism to the next. These differences

Step-by-Step Chart

	Growing a Tomato Plant
Steps	**Details**
1. Gather the materials you will need.	Materials: tomato seeds, soil, water, fertilizer, insecticide, a "cage" to support the growing vines, plastic to keep plants safe from frost, shovel or hoe, flowerpot if starting the plants indoors.
2. Plant the seeds.	Plant the seeds about three feet (0.9 m) apart in a sunny area. Add fertilizer to help the plants grow. If it is early spring, you may need to place a plastic tent over the plants to keep them safe from frost.
3. Care for the young plants.	Pick weeds before they can harm the small plants. Water daily when there is no rain. Fertilizer may be added to help the plants grow. When the plants get larger, they may need cages for support. Use insecticides to kill pests.
4. Harvest the tomatoes.	Pick the tomatoes when they are red and firm. Not all tomatoes will ripen at the same time. Check the plant and pick ripe tomatoes every one to two days.

A step-by-step chart illustrates the sequence in which to perform an act. In the step-by-step chart above, we learn how to bring a living thing, a tomato plant, from seed to harvest following the four steps.

Plants

become evident when comparing and contrasting the plant and animal kingdoms. In this chapter, we will explore the lives of plants to find out how they remain alive. In the following chapter, we will do the same for animals.

Nutrition in Plants

All plants are autotrophs, which means "self-feeder." Autotrophic organisms create food by combining elements in the environment with the aid of an energy source. When that source is light from the sun, the process is known as photosynthesis. Plants create their own food through photosynthesis.

A substance in plants known as chlorophyll—the substance that gives plants their green color—gathers energy in the form of sunlight. Plants use sunlight to change carbon dioxide and water into glucose, which is a form of sugar that plants use as food. Oxygen

Sequence Chart: Photosynthesis

1: Plants take in water from the soil.

2: Plants take in carbon dioxide from the air.

3: Chlorophyll in plants takes in sunlight.

4: Plants combine the carbon dioxide, water, and sunlight to form glucose (a food source) and oxygen (a waste product).

5: Plants store the glucose to use later.

6: Plants release oxygen into the air.

A sequence chart, such as the one above, shows the major steps in a process. This chart shows the six primary steps in photosynthesis.

Looking at Differences Between Living and Nonliving Things with Graphic Organizers

is a waste product of photosynthesis. Transport plays an important role in healthy nutrition, since both raw materials and waste materials must cross through cell walls.

Tree Diagram: Transport in Plants

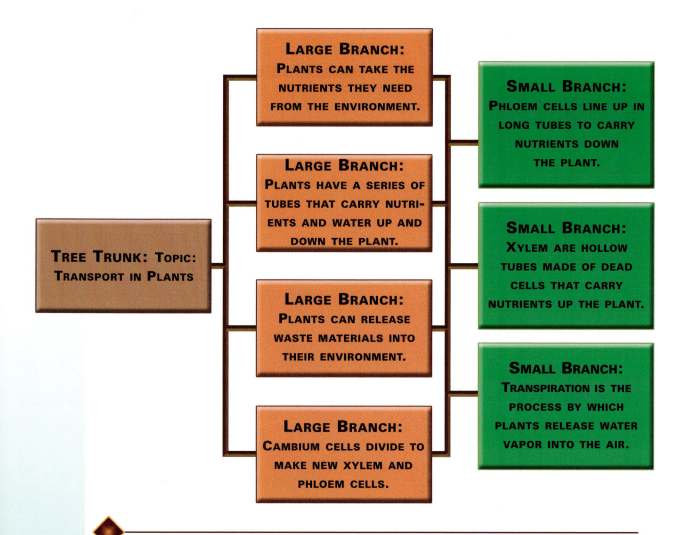

A tree diagram uses an outline of a tree, with its trunk and branches, to illustrate the hierarchy of a system. In this case, transport in plants is illustrated, with its primary processes being the largest part of the tree, the trunk. The secondary processes, which are supported by the primary process, form the branches.

Transport in Plants

Plants are capable of taking nutrients in from their environment. Waste materials such as oxygen are eliminated with the aid of small openings on the surfaces of leaves. Plants release water vapor into the air through a process called transpiration.

Plants also have several methods of transporting nutrients throughout their bodies. All plants have a series of tubes that carry water, nutrients, and waste materials up and down the plant. Plants do not need a pump like the heart. Instead, their roots, stems, and leaves have special abilities to transport food and water.

Xylem are dead, rigid cells that provide support for a plant. They form hollow tubes that extend up the length of the stem and branches. The tubes that xylem form carry water and nutrients upward from the soil. Phloem are plant cells that line up in long tubes to transport food down the plant. Between the xylem and phloem are a third type of cell, called cambium. Cambium cells carry out cell division to make new xylem and phloem cells.

Respiration in Plants

Just like all living creatures, plants need energy to carry out their life processes. During photosynthesis, plants make their own food source by combining carbon dioxide with water, releasing oxygen in the process. When plants need energy, they take oxygen from the air and combine it with some of the glucose they created during photosynthesis. This is called cellular respiration. Plants use the energy that is released for many purposes, including growth, regulation, and even photosynthesis.

Synthesis and Growth in Plants

Most plants start life as a tiny seed that contains genetic material and food. As a seed begins to sprout, it takes in nutrients from the soil, and from the air and sun when it breaks free of the soil. Plants use these nutrients to synthesize more cells. The synthesis of cellulose allows the plant to grow larger and stronger.

Plants grow larger as cell division takes place. Plants also grow larger as a result of the expansion of cells. Most plants grow throughout their entire life. An oak tree begins life as a tiny acorn, and continues to grow for the duration of its life.

Excretion in Plants

Most plants excrete far less waste material than animals. Plants often store waste materials. When a plant has too much carbon dioxide, it may store it for later use in special cells called vacuoles. Oxygen and water are the waste products of photosynthesis, and the leaves of plants allow oxygen to pass out of the plant and into the air around it. Some plants may also store waste material in parts that will eventually die and drop off, such as the leaves of trees that turn color and drop off in the autumn, or the stems of flowering plants that die and regrow in the spring from a bulb planted under the soil.

One way that plants, such as this potato blossom, react to their environments is by turning their leaves to the sun. This process is called heliotropism, which means sun seeking, and allows the plant to absorb as much sunlight as possible.

Regulation in Plants

Regulation in plants is much less complex than it is in animals. Plants are not able to react to their surroundings as animals can. That does not mean, however, that they are incapable of regulating their existence to improve their chances of survival. For example, some plants can react to touch. Some ferns are capable of folding their leaves in an attempt to protect them from predators. Some vines wave about with the wind searching for something solid to wrap themselves around for support.

POTATO PLANT DIAGRAM

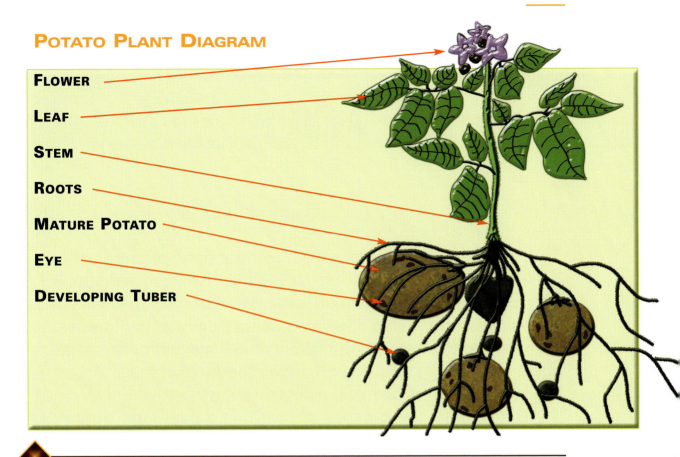

Shown here is a diagram of a potato plant. The potato plant is a perfect subject for a diagram since half of the plant, the half that bears the potatoes, is underground and unable to be seen in a photograph.

REPRODUCTION IN PLANTS

Plants use a variety of methods to produce offspring. Some plants, such as the potato plant, can reproduce sexually and asexually. The flowers of the potato plant attract insects, which carry pollen to other potato plants. A speck of pollen is the male cell, and it joins with a female cell, or egg, of another plant. The fertilized egg grows into a seed.

As the potato plant grows, it stores food in its roots. Eventually this food forms a large lump called a tuber. If left to mature, the tubers themselves can undergo asexual reproduction and form new plants. The "eyes" on potatoes are actually new organisms budding off of the parent potato.

Chapter Four

Animals

All animals are heterotrophs. "Heterotroph" means "other feeding." Heterotrophs ingest organic matter to meet their nutritional needs. Ingestion is the taking in of food. Most animals have a mouth that allows nutrients from the environment to enter the organism's body. Many also have teeth and saliva, which help to mechanically break the food into smaller pieces. This is known as mechanical digestion.

Digestion is the process of breaking down large organic molecules into molecules that are small enough to pass through cell walls. These molecules provide a source of energy for an animal's cells and help to regulate the other life processes. They also help to build new cells and repair damaged cells. Animals digest materials with the aid of a variety of enzymes, which are substances made by organs in the body.

Egestion is the elimination of unused organic material. This happens on the cellular level as waste products pass through cell walls and enter the bloodstream. It also occurs

Heterotrophs, such as this hippopotamus, have large mouths and teeth to help digest their food.

KWL Chart: Plants and Animals

What I Know	What I Want to Know	What I Learned
Plants are autotrophs, which means they make their own food.	Are animals autotrophs? Or are they something different?	Animals are heterotrophs, which means they eat organic matter to meet their nutritional needs.
Plants have tubes within them that transport water and nutrients where they are needed.	Do animals have these same structures?	Animals have either an open or closed system of tubes called vessels. The vessels transport blood, water, and nutrients where they are needed.
Plants rely on cellular respiration to make the energy they need for life processes.	How is respiration different in animals?	Animals are capable of two forms of cellular respiration: aerobic and anaerobic.
Most plants continue to synthesize new cells and grow larger as long as they are alive.	Are synthesis and growth the same in animals?	Animals stop growing at a certain age, but they continue to synthesize new cells to repair damaged ones for their entire lives.
Plants are capable of ridding themselves of waste materials, but they often store waste materials in their bodies.	Do animals store or excrete waste materials?	Animals excrete waste materials with the aid of the bloodstream, kidneys, bladder, and lungs.
In rare cases, some plants can react to touch, allowing them to improve their chances of survival.	How does regulation in animals compare to regulation in plants?	Regulation in animals is often more complex and varied, and includes the fight-or-flight response.
Many plants are capable of asexual and sexual reproduction.	How do animals reproduce?	Although animals have developed numerous methods of reproduction, only a few animals, such as the hydra, can reproduce asexually.

KWL charts do a good job of showing you how to take the information you've already learned and apply it to future knowledge. The chart asks you what you already know. Then it asks you what you would like to know. Based on what you already know, the chart helps you answer this question.

when the body eliminates undigested organic material in the form of feces.

TRANSPORT IN ANIMALS

Most animals have a system of vessels and organs that transports nutrients and other materials around their bodies. Human beings, like many other animals, have a circulatory system made up of blood, blood vessels, and the heart. Our circulatory system transports oxygen, water, nutrients from digested food, and waste materials. It also transports chemicals from the organs that create and store them to the organs and cells where they are needed. This type of system is called a closed circulatory system because the blood and chemicals are transported within a closed system of vessels and organs.

Some less complex animals, such as insects, have an open circulatory system. In these creatures, materials that need to be transported about the organism are not always enclosed within vessels. Blood sometimes enters open areas between organs called sinuses. As blood enters a sinus, it surrounds the tissues there, allowing the free transport of nutrients and waste materials across cell membranes.

RESPIRATION IN ANIMALS

In animals, breathing is an important part of respiration. Breathing moves oxygen into the lungs and carbon dioxide out of the lungs. However, respiration is actually much more than breathing. Cellular respiration creates energy by breaking food down. Animal cells accomplish this by combining oxygen and glucose. Glucose is the substance that plants create during photosynthesis. Energy is stored in the molecular bonds of glucose. During cellular respiration, animals use oxygen to tear down glucose, releasing the energy stored within its molecular bonds. This whole process is monitored by chemicals in the organism called enzymes.

Comparison Chart: Respiration in Animals

Lung	Gill	Trachea
A lung is a sacklike organ that allows some animals to breathe.	A gill is a thin, tissuelike organ that allows many aquatic animals to breathe.	A trachea is a narrow tube that allows many kinds of insects to breathe.
An animal's lungs fill with air when the animal inhales.	An animal with gills takes water in through the mouth, forces it over gills, and then out through long slits that are usually on the animal's neck.	Animals with tracheae take air into their bodies through tiny holes called spiracles.
When the lungs fill with air, oxygen passes through thin tissues in the lungs into the bloodstream.	Oxygen in the water passes through the thin membranes of the gills, and then into the bloodstream.	Air travels through the tracheae and into smaller tubes and organs.
Carbon dioxide—a waste product of cellular respiration—moves from the bloodstream into the lungs.	Carbon dioxide passes from the bloodstream through the gills.	The smallest tracheae allow cells to exchange oxygen, carbon dioxide, and water.
When an animal exhales, carbon dioxide leaves the lungs and becomes a part of the air.	Carbon dioxide is flushed out of the animal as it forces water through its gill openings.	Carbon dioxide exits the body through the tracheae and spiracles.
		Some insects, like the grasshopper, have air sacs that control the flow of air through their tracheae.

Within the animal kingdom, there are different structures designed to take oxygen out of the air, allowing animals to breathe. Three of these structures—lungs, gills, and tracheae—are listed on the comparison chart above.

Cellular respiration that is dependent upon oxygen is called aerobic respiration. During increased activity, the lungs and circulatory system work quicker to bring more oxygen to the cells for aerobic respiration. When the cells cannot get enough oxygen, they begin to break glucose down into a substance called lactic acid. This process, called anaerobic respiration, quickly causes soreness in the muscles and shortness of breath.

SYNTHESIS AND GROWTH IN ANIMALS

Animals begin life as a single-celled egg. Some animals, such as human beings, grow within the mother's body. Many creatures, including birds, insects, and some reptiles, grow within an egg shell outside of the mother's body. The single cell attains nourishment from its surroundings. The cell uses this nourishment to synthesize the materials necessary for growth. Cell division occurs rapidly, especially at first. As the organism increases in size, it begins to synthesize different types of cells, each of which has a different function. Some types of animals molt their outer coverings as they grow. Eventually, the organism takes on the appearance of its parents. Unlike plants, animals grow only for a part of their lives, even though they continue to synthesize new cells to repair damaged ones for the rest of their lives.

EXCRETION IN ANIMALS

During cellular respiration in animals, cells obtain energy from the oxidation of food molecules. This process results in the creation of water and carbon dioxide, both of which are the waste products of cellular respiration. Water and unused substances are carried from the cells via the circulatory system to the kidneys. From there, the water is excreted from the body through the bladder. The circulatory system transports carbon dioxide away from the cells and into the lungs, where it is excreted into the air when an animal exhales. Most animals are also capable of excreting waste materials through openings in the skin. Human beings do this when they

Idea Wheel: Excretion in Human Beings

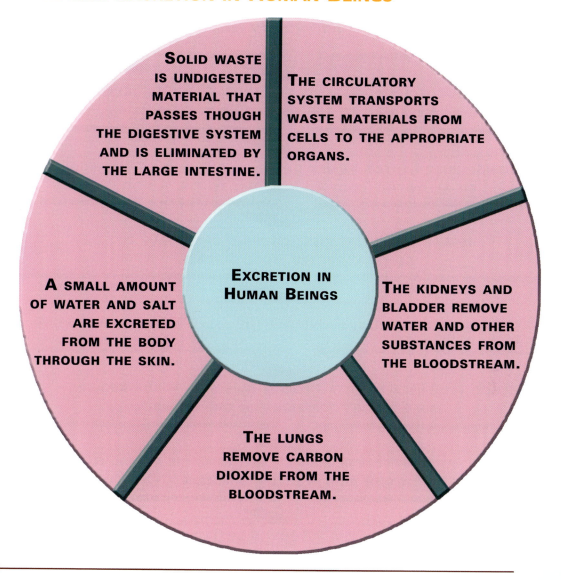

The idea wheel shown here features the subject of excretion in animals and the subcategories that surround it. Idea wheels are used to help stimulate discussion on complex topics.

sweat. Solid waste is undigested matter that is eliminated from the body via an animal's digestive system. Simple animals, though, may use a less complex method of excretion.

Regulation in Animals

In more complex animals, regulation is usually conducted by the nervous system and the endocrine system. The nervous system is

SEQUENCE CHART: FIGHT OR FLIGHT

> **THE ANIMAL IS FACED WITH A POTENTIALLY LIFE-THREATENING SITUATION.**

> **THE NERVOUS SYSTEM ASSESSES THE THREAT AND QUICKLY SENDS MESSAGES TO THE ENDOCRINE SYSTEM.**

> **THE ENDOCRINE SYSTEM PUMPS OUT HIGHER LEVELS OF CHEMICALS TO ALLOW THE BODY TO RESPOND TO THE THREAT.**

> **HEART RATE INCREASES, CAUSING CHEMICALS TO BE TRANSPORTED MORE QUICKLY.**

> **BREATHING RATE INCREASES, PROVIDING THE CELLS WITH EXTRA OXYGEN.**

> **BLOOD FLOW IS REDIRECTED TO THE MUSCLES, WHICH REQUIRE MORE ENERGY FOR FIGHTING OR FLEEING.**

> **PERCEPTION OF PAIN DECREASES, ALLOWING THE ANIMAL TO IGNORE PAIN IN FAVOR OF ACTION.**

> **IN VERY LITTLE TIME, THE ANIMAL'S BODY IS BETTER PREPARED TO FIGHT OFF THE THREAT, OR TO FLEE FROM THE THREAT.**

This sequence chart illustrates the series of events that take place within an animal as a response to life-threatening situations. When an animal is threatened, the fight-or-flight response kicks into action, resulting in a series of biological changes that occur almost instantaneously.

made up of the brain and the nerves. The endocrine system is made up of a system of glands, such as the thyroid and pituitary glands, and chemicals known as hormones. These systems help to regulate the life processes of the organism in numerous ways.

When faced with a dangerous situation, animals experience the "fight or flight" response. When threatened, the nervous system prompts the glands of the endocrine system to pump higher levels of chemicals into the bloodstream. These chemicals cause several changes in the organism's body, including increased breathing and heart rate, a redirection of blood flow to the muscles, and a temporary desensitization to pain. These changes better equip an animal to defend itself in a dangerous situation or to flee from it.

Bullfrogs, such as the one shown here, lay their eggs in still bodies of water. The eggs then hatch into tadpoles, which incubate in the water anywhere from one to two years.

REPRODUCTION IN ANIMALS

Animals have developed numerous methods for reproducing. The majority of animals reproduce sexually, although some simple animals, such as the hydra, mentioned earlier, reproduce by budding. Some animals, such as humans, usually fertilize a single egg at a time and have a single offspring. The new life-form matures within the mother's body. Other animals, however, can have two or more babies at a time. Birds, insects, and many reptiles lay eggs, which they either care for or leave to fend for themselves.

Some animals, such as the bullfrog, can lay tens of thousands of eggs at one time. Female bullfrogs lay up to 20,000 eggs in mats that float on the surface of a body of water. The male bullfrog then fertilizes the eggs. You might wonder why bullfrogs, since they lay so many eggs, haven't taken over the world yet. Adult bullfrogs do not care for the eggs, and many of them end up as lunch for other species.

Chapter Five

The Balance of Nature

The bodies of all living things are miniature factories constantly processing materials to create power. In order to keep functioning properly, all factories need raw materials with which to work. Other factories and businesses affect the way a single factory functions. Likewise, a single factory can have a profound influence on outside entities. In short, a factory simply cannot function without interacting with the outside world.

Factory Diagram

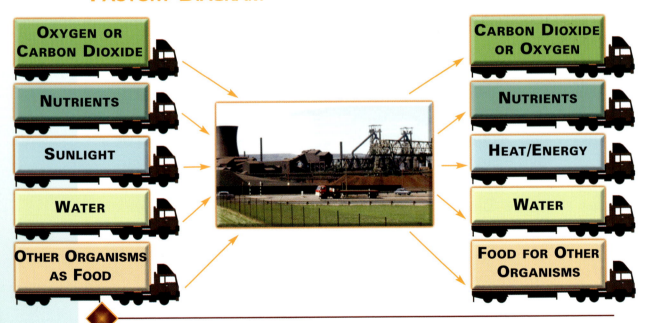

A factory diagram illustrates what goes into a system and what goes out. The factory is any type of system. In this case, the factory is a living organism. In order to survive, the organism, much like a factory, needs resources from the environment.

The Balance of Nature

Living things depend upon each other in many ways to maintain homeostasis. Many animals use other living things as a food source. Parasites, for instance, are creatures that live on or in another creature, gaining sustenance from a host creature's body. Without the process of photosynthesis in plants, all life would perish. Plants depend on animals for carbon dioxide as much as animals depend on plants for oxygen. However, neither plants nor animals could survive were it not for the carbon dioxide and oxygen that they continuously trade back and forth. Oxygen and carbon dioxide are just two of the many nonliving things that living things interact with all the time.

Earthworms, such as this one, are everywhere, and they help maintain the balance of nature in many ways, including enriching the soil. However, they need to take nutrients from the environment in order to do this.

Environments

The reason living things are alive is because they are capable of all seven life processes. These processes take place within the organism, in an area scientists sometimes refer to as the interior environment. Everything outside a living thing's body is that organism's exterior environment, or simply its environment. An organism's environment is everything that surrounds it and affects the way it lives.

An earthworm's environment isn't just the soil it squirms through. It also includes water, minerals, air, sunlight, and even other organisms—dead as well as alive. The earthworm needs these nonliving things in order to survive, as do many other subterranean creatures. Earthworms take the nutrients they need to live from their environment, but they give back beneficial things to the environment. The tunnels they dig help plants by making room for their roots to grow. They also help to break down dead organisms, leaving the soil rich and fertile. Other animals, such as birds and rodents, eat worms to stay alive. These organisms' environments simply would not be the same without the earthworm.

Spider Map: The Earthworm's Environment

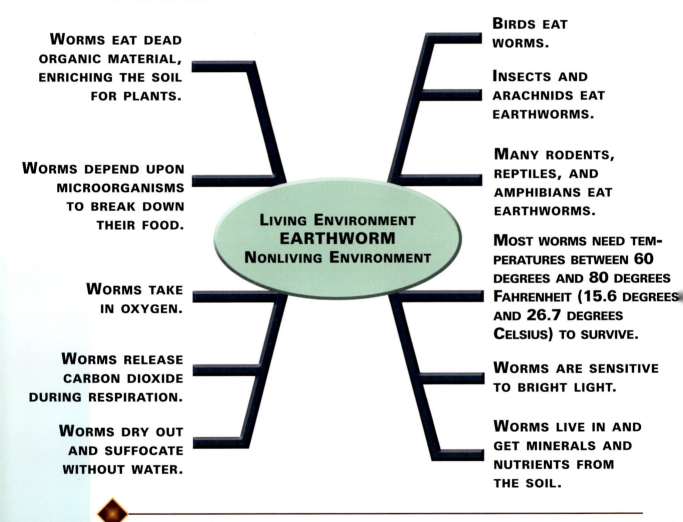

This spider map shows the living and nonliving components of the earthworm's environment. Worms eat things in the living environment. Likewise, they are eaten by other living things. From the nonliving environment, worms need such essentials as oxygen and water.

Ecosystems

An ecosystem is a complex series of interactions and relationships within an environment. You could think of it as a complex web connecting all the living and nonliving things that interact with each other on a daily basis. An ecosystem is sometimes easier to understand by looking at a small section of it. Food chains and food webs show how organisms in an ecosystem depend on each other for sustenance. In an ecosystem, energy is constantly being transferred from one part to another. Organic matter is recycled as organisms are eaten or as they die and decompose.

The organisms in an ecosystem can be categorized as producers, consumers, and decomposers. Each type of creature depends on the others for life. Producers use energy from the sun to create their own food. They sustain the rest of the ecosystem with the energy they pass on to the organisms that consume them. Plants are the main producers in any ecosystem.

Consumers get their food from their environment. Many animals eat plants. The energy that plants create is transferred to the living things that feed on them. Many animals eat animals that have eaten plants. Primary consumers are those that eat plants for energy. Secondary consumers eat primary consumers. Tertiary consumers eat primary and secondary consumers. Sometimes secondary and tertiary consumers also eat plants. A simple food chain can help to illustrate the relationship among consumers in an ecosystem.

Decomposers such as fungi and bacteria get their energy by eating dead organisms and organic waste products. Decomposers break these things down into the basic nutrients, which return to the soil. Producers then use the nutrients to make their own food.

Ecosystems have been recycling matter in this way for millions of years. In fact, the plants and animals of an ecosystem are made up of the same molecules that once made up the creatures living in the past. Those same molecules will "build" the living

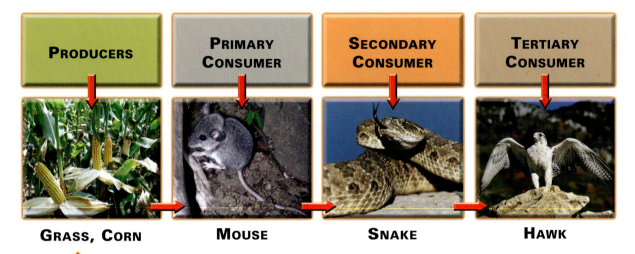

The food chain diagram illustrates the sequence in which one animal eats another. Here, the producers are eaten by the primary consumer, the mouse. The mouse is then eaten by the secondary consumer, the snake, which, in turn, is eaten by the hawk, the tertiary consumer.

organisms of the future. Energy, on the other hand, is constantly flowing through an ecosystem. Plants use energy in the form of sunlight to combine nutrients and make food. Animals eat the plants and break them down into useful nutrients, releasing energy in the process.

BIOMES AND ADAPTATIONS

Earth is covered with many different types of regional ecosystems called biomes. Each biome is defined by its major form of plant life and its climate. While scientists sometimes disagree about the number of biomes on Earth, the following list is generally accepted as comprehensive: tundras, coniferous forests, deciduous forests, grasslands, savannas, deserts, chaparrals, tropical rain forests, and tropical seasonal forests. Biomes are often divided into subcategories of similar regions. Many scientists consider Earth's underwater regions to be a single biome, while others break it down into subcategories such as lake, ocean, river, and so on.

Two biomes of the same type can be located on opposite sides of the world. Since they share the same climate, they often develop similar types of fauna. The prairies of North America and the steppes of Asia, for example, are both grassland biomes, and they both feature similar types of wildlife.

The living things of a biome are well adapted to life in that area of the world. Adaptations allow the many species of an ecosystem to survive and flourish. Living things cannot thrive as a species unless they develop the traits necessary to live in their particular biome. The Arctic polar bear would have a difficult time in the rain forest with its heavy, white pelt. That trait developed as the polar bear adapted to its tundra surrounding. The poison dart frog of Central America could not live in the tundra, but it thrives in the rain forests because that is the biome to which it has adapted.

No two organisms are identical. This is a result of sexual reproduction and the variations that it creates. Those organisms that are better adapted to their environment have a greater chance of survival. Organisms that do not receive beneficial adaptations from their parents usually die off because they have not been properly equipped with the tools they need to survive. Over time, whole species develop the adaptations that help to protect their existence in their particular biome. Other traits disappear because they are not needed for survival or they are detrimental to survival. This process is known as evolution.

THE BALANCE OF NATURE

The living organisms in an ecosystem depend on one another for life in many ways. Living creatures form a balance of nature. Keeping this balance is necessary for living things. It is only by interacting with its environment that a species can survive. Millions of interactions are necessary within an ecosystem to create a balance between the myriad of living things and their nonliving counterparts.

GLOSSARY

amoeba A single-celled organism that has no specific form and moves using a pseudopod, or "false foot."
archaea Single-celled creatures that live in extreme environments.
botanist A scientist who studies plants.
chaparral A biome marked by hot summers, cool winters, and evergreen shrubs.
compound microscope A tool that uses multiple lenses to magnify very small objects.
enzymes Chemicals in the body that help carry out biological processes.
fertilize To combine a male sperm cell with a female egg cell to create new life.
homeostasis An organism's ability to keep its internal environment stable despite external stimuli.
hormones Chemicals in the body that help carry out biological processes.
molt To shed skin, feathers, or an outer shell during growth.
Monera The kingdom of living things that includes bacteria and archaea.
organelle A structure inside a cell that fulfills a specific function.
organic Relating to living things.
parasite A creature that lives on or in another organism and depends on its host for survival.
physicist A scientist who specializes in physics.

physiologist A scientist who studies the functions of living things and their parts.

Protista The kingdom of living things that includes single-celled and simple multicelled creatures.

protozoa A large group of single-celled organisms, including the amoeba.

stimulus Anything that causes a response.

taxonomy The classification of living things in an ordered system.

transpiration The process in plants of releasing water vapor into the air through holes in the leaves.

vacuole A small structure inside a cell that stores food, water, or waste material.

FOR MORE INFORMATION

The American Institute of Biological Sciences
1444 I Street NW, Suite 200
Washington, DC 20005
(202) 628-1500
Web site: http://www.aibs.org/core/index.html

The American Society for Cell Biology
8120 Woodmont Avenue, Suite 750
Bethesda, MD 20814-2762
(301) 347-9300
Web site: http://www.ascb.org
e-mail: ascbinfo@ascb.org

WEB SITES

Due to the changing nature of Internet links, the Rosen Publishing Group, Inc., has developed an online list of Web sites related to the subject of this book. This site is updated regularly. Please use this link to access the list:

http://www.rosenlinks.com/ugosle/dbgo

For Further Reading

Baeuerle, Patrick A., and Norbert Landa. *The Cell Works*. Hauppauge, NY: Barron's Educational Series, 1998.

Campbell, Neil. *Biology: Exploring Life*. Upper Saddle River, NJ: Pearson Prentice Hall, 2003.

Padilla, Michael J., et al. *Science Explorer: Animals*. Upper Saddle River, NJ: Pearson Prentice Hall, 2001.

Padilla, Michael J., et al. *Science Explorer: From Bacteria to Plants*. Upper Saddle River, NJ: Pearson Prentice Hall, 2000.

Spilsbury, Louise, and Richard Spilsbury. *Food Chains and Webs: From Producers to Decomposers*. Port Melbourne, Australia: Heinemann Library, 2004.

Strauss, Rochelle. *Tree of Life: The Incredible Biodiversity of Life on Earth*. Buffalo, NY: Kids Can Press, 2004.

VanCleave, Janice Pratt. *Biology for Every Kid: 101 Easy Experiments That Really Work*. Indianapolis, IN: Wiley Publishers, Inc., 1999.

Walker, Richard. *Microscopic Life*. Boston, MA: Houghton Mifflin, 2004.

Bibliography

Burnie, David. *Life* (Eyewitness Science). New York, NY: Dorling Kindersley, 1990.

Kraus, David. *Concepts in Modern Biology*. Upper Saddle River, NJ: Globe Fearon Educational Publishers, 1999.

Mallery, Charles. "Cell Theory." University of Miami Department of Biology. May 14, 2003. Retrieved April 27, 2005 (http://fig.cox.miami.edu/~cmallery/150/unity/cell.text.htm).

McShaffrey, Dave. "Environmental Biology—Ecosystems." Marietta College. January 10, 2005. Retrieved April 27, 2005 (http:// www.marietta.edu/~biol/102/ecosystem.html#RolesofOrganisms2).

Pullen, Stephanie, ed. "The Tundra Biome." University of California, Berkeley. April 2004. Retrieved April 28, 2005 (http://www.ucmp.berkeley.edu/glossary/gloss5/biome/tundra.html).

Walker, Richard. *Encyclopedia of the Human Body*. New York, NY: Dorling Kindersley, 2002.

Wikipedia. "Linnaean Taxonomy." April 23, 2005. Retrieved April 27, 2005 (http://en.wikipedia.org/wiki/Linnaean_taxonomy).

Woodward, Susan L. "Introduction to Biomes." Radford University. Retrieved April 24, 2004 (http://www.radford.edu/~swoodwar/CLASSES/GEOG235/biomes/intro.html).

World Book Multimedia Encylopedia. CD-ROM. Chicago, IL: World Book, 1998.

Index

A
archaea, 12–13

B
bacteria, 5, 12, 13, 15
biomes, 40–41

C
cambium cells, 25
carbon dioxide, 12, 23, 25, 26, 30, 32, 37
cell division, 12, 18, 25, 26, 32
cells, plant and animal, 10–12
cell theory, 7–9
cellular respiration, 11, 25, 30, 32
 aerobic and anaerobic, 32
cellulose, 12, 25
crystals, 16

D
digestion, 28

E
ecosystems, 39–40, 41
egestion, 28–30
eight traits, 16–20
energy, 39, 40
environment(s), 37–38, 39
evolution, 41

F
food chain, 39

G
glucose, 23, 30, 32

H
heterotroph, 28
homeostasis, 21, 37
Hooke, Robert, 7

K
kingdoms of life, 14–15

L
lactic acid, 32
Leeuwenhoek, Antonie van, 8

M
metabolism, 20

O
oxygen, 10, 12, 23–24, 25, 26, 30, 32, 37

P
parasites, 37
photosynthesis, 12, 23–24, 25, 26, 30, 37
protists, 13

R
reproduction, 12, 16, 18–19, 27, 35, 41

S
Schleiden, Matthias, 9
Schwann, Theodor, 9
seven life processes, 16, 37

single-celled organisms, 5, 12–13, 17, 18, 20

T
taxonomy, 14, 15

tests, 6
transpiration, 25

V
viruses, 16

About the Author

Greg Roza graduated from State University of New York Fredonia in 1997 with a masters degree in English. Since then he has worked as a writer and editor of educational materials. Greg has written several books on the topic of living things. He has also helped develop several sources of graphic organizers on a variety of topics, including science, history, math, and language arts.

Photo Credits

Cover, p. 1, 4–5, 15, 28, 36, 40 © Royalty-Free/Nova Development Corporation; p. 7 courtesy of Tahara Anderson; pp. (graphics), 8, 9, 11, 13, 14, 16, 19, 21, 22, 23, 24, 27, 29, 31, 33, 34, 38 courtesy of Nelson Sá; p. 20 © Lester V. Bergman/Corbis; p. 26 © Richard Hamilton Smith/Corbis; p. 35 © Joe McDonald/Corbis; p. 37 © Eric and David Hosking/Corbis.

Designer: Nelson Sá; Editor: Nicholas Croce; Photo Researcher: Nelson Sá

400X4 Looking at differences between . . .